Story Dog

For my Cal.
And for anyone, big or small,
who has ever opened their heart to a rescue animal.
You're beautiful. J.F.

SIMON & SCHUSTER
First published in Great Britain in 2023 by Simon & Schuster UK Ltd
1st Floor, 222 Gray's Inn Road, London WC1X 8HB

Text and illustrations copyright © Jan Fearnley 2023
The right of Jan Fearnley to be identified as the author
and illustrator of this work has been asserted by her in accordance
with the Copyright, Designs and Patents Act, 1988

A CIP catalogue record for this book is available from
the British Library upon request

ISBN: 978-1-4711-9176-3 (HB)
ISBN: 978-1-4711-9175-6 (PB)
ISBN: 978-1-4711-9174-9 (eBook)

Printed in China
1 3 5 7 9 10 8 6 4 2

Story Dog

JAN FEARNLEY

SIMON & SCHUSTER

London   New York   Sydney   Toronto   New Delhi

I'm Harry. I love stories, but they make me nervous. When it's my turn to read out loud in class, my voice shakes.

The words jumble and tumble.
I make so many mistakes.

I wish I were a better reader.

After school, I go to the dogs home.
My Mam works there three days a week.

I sit in the back of the office
and I practise reading my book.

The dogs at the shelter don't know
why they are there.

Some bark and cry at the fence.
Some jump around and wag their tails
and they have big smiley brown eyes.

They're the ones who always find
their forever home first.

"Look at this sad old dog," says Mam.
"His name is Cal. He needs a friend."
He doesn't bark or run around or wag his tail.

He sits in the corner, silently waiting for his
family . . . who never come.
He stares into space with his sad black eyes.

"Can I take him for a walk?" I say.
So off we go together,
me and this sad old dog.

At first he doesn't know me –
but he likes my sandwich.

This is how we become friends.
Every day after school, me and old Cal
walk together, while he waits for his family.

He likes the track in the wood . . .

He likes the big meadow.

We chase shadows and jump on the rocks.
Cal has the rest of my sandwich.

Then he sniffs at my book.

Oh, my! He wants me
to read him a story!

My throat feels tight
and my hands begin
to sweat.

He nudges the book,
and tilts his head, ready to listen.

Oh, my.

With the old dog sitting at
my side, slowly I begin . . .

I make some mistakes,

but Cal doesn't mind a bit.

He leans closer and rests
his nose on my book . . .
He just wants me
to keep trying,

so I do . . .

And the more I read, with his big
old nose at the bottom of the page,

the words become easier to say . . .

Cal's old eyes twinkle.
He likes the story.

WOOF! Well done!
Let's read it again!

Second time is easier.

With his head cocked to one side, he listens to me,
his long ears flopped down like two old slippers.

Is he smiling?

He likes it –

he likes it when I read!

And the words fly out of my mouth.
I can say them! I can read!

So every day, we go for our walk and we find a good place for our picnic and our book. We are lost in our stories . . .

Sometimes we're pirates!

Fabulous bakers.

Racing car drivers!

Amazing trapeze perfomers!

He is the best teacher, this old dog.

At the end of the story,
I close the book.

We have to go back now.

"Bye, then. See you tomorrow."

How I wish I could take him home with me!

The next day, I read out loud in class.
I imagine old Cal listening.
I'm brave and I try hard.

I get a sticker for
excellent reading.
I can't wait to show Cal!

But at the shelter the manager is waiting for me.

There is some news.

Cal has found a family.

And he's leaving today.

I want to say "Great!" but the words are hard to find.

"He likes stories and sandwiches," I say.

I hope they'll read him stories.

I hope they'll love him.

I head to the office to collect my things.
I'm mixed-up happy and sad.

Oh, I'll miss that old dog so much!

It's time to go home.
The walk to the car feels ever so long.
My eyes and face are hot, my books feel heavy.

But as I turn the corner, people are waiting.
It's Mam and the shelter manager,
and beside them . . . is an old dog.

A dog with black eyes, and big ears that
flop down like two old slippers! CAL!

"Haven't you forgotten someone?" Mam smiles.
"He likes stories and sandwiches.
Now let's take your dog home."

We jump in the car, the black eyes twinkle.

WOOF!

And off we go home,
the three of us –

me and Mam and our lovely old dog . . .

to begin a new story . . .

DOGGY 1

. . . together.